Nina's song
A Story by Lori

Lori Fitzgerald

with illustrations by
Teresa J. Knight

ISBN: 9781794379329

One sunshiney June morning, I opened up the blinds and can you guess who I spotted there, in the window box? **Nina!**
She was hiding in the pink and purple petunias!

Only, I didn't know her name at that time.
She was a cute little pink and white creature, all
huddled up so that she might look like a tiny
garden ornament.
I watched her try not to be seen. She sat so still and
quiet for the longest time!

I knew I couldn't let the cats go out for they would
likely chase her away. And so I left for the day, with
Stella and Bailey in the window looking doleful and
just in front of them, on the outside, was Nina, quietly
huddled in the pink and purple flowers.

The next morning, Nina was still there. Once again I watched her stay very still. And once again I couldn't put the cats out for fear they might scare the little creature away. I put a little dish of water on the window sill in case she was thirsty.

By the third day, Bailey and Stella absolutely HAD to go and play outside. And so I found a cardboard box and carefully poked some holes in it and placed newspaper in the bottom. Then I gently grabbed Nina with a cloth. She squealed. I quickly put her in the box and closed the lid.

Then I let the cats out.

I kept Nina's box in the guest bedroom, to keep her safe. She must be very hungry, I thought, and so I offered her various foods: nuts, seeds, a crunchy biscuit - Nina ate everything!

That evening, I went in to visit her. When I opened up the box, the little creature had made her very own house inside it by ripping tiny strips of newspaper and weaving them together.

The house now had a doorway, and windows - it was amazing!

Nina blinked up at me and squiggled her whiskers. She looked very house-proud!

I asked the neighbours on my street if they had lost a gerbil by any chance but they all said no, they had not. And so that was when I named my gerbil "Nina".

I bought a book on the care of gerbils. I learned that they are friendly, clever animals that love to play.   They like to stand up on their hind legs when not moving about. They have tails that are as long as their bodies. And they love to eat all kinds of grain, and pasta! Just like my Nina!

Then some of my neighbours who hadn't lost their gerbil came over to visit Nina.

"THAT," said Mr. Neighbour knowingly, "is NOT a gerbil. THAT is a Rat."

Nina couldn't help looking guilty.

"A rat," I breathed. Oh no.

"Rats," said my neighbour, "are vile, disgusting creatures. They carry diseases. They'll over-run you in no time. You need to Get Rid of It."

I looked down at little pink-nosed Nina, her white whiskers clean and twitching, sitting in front of the tiny house she had built for herself. I didn't think she looked either vile or disgusting. She certainly didn't look as though she were about to over-run the established order of things.

I did however worry about diseases and not just for Nina's sake but for Bailey and Stella and my dogs. And so next day I took Nina in her box to see a vet who specializes in the care of rodents.

Nina was scared. She peed a little. She regarded the vet with suspicion. But she was a very good patient and she didn't bite him.

I asked the vet if Nina had any diseases.
"No," he said. Then he added: "She is beautiful."

Though she didn't have a bushy tail like a squirrel or a bobtail like a bunny, my Nina was beautiful!

My Nina was beautiful!

And it became official: I was caregiver to a beautiful white rat!

I bought a book about the care of rats.

I learned they are every bit as funny and clever and sweet as gerbils. They are loyal and love to climb. They enjoy cuddles!

Despite their sweet tooth, they shouldn't eat too much candy, no matter what they might tell you!

Eventually I made Nina an even bigger house cut out of an apple box and I put her own little house inside it for her. When I offered her tissues to play with, she took them and made them into curtains! Had she added a front porch and a swing set, I wouldn't have been in the least bit surprised.

She loved to lay in a sunbeam, or to snuggle on my shoulder and nibble on my hair and she never ever bit me.

She loved to lay in a sunbeam

I went away for a holiday and left Nina and the others in the care of a gentle, loving pet-sitter. What I didn't know was that this woman had a deep dislike of rats.

Nina did not approve of being spoken to in unkind terms and bit the woman's finger. While I was sincerely sorry and I told the pet-sitter so, I couldn't help being proud of my Nina for making her feelings known!

Little rats often have trouble breathing and so I made certain that there was steam in her room from time to time to help her.

When she had skin problems I found that she shouldn't be having seeds or nuts any more - they were too fatty for her.

And my Nina lived to a good age for a little rat. She had good food, good care, and though she never said so, I think she knew she was loved.

I think she knew she was loved

Nina's Song

(This was the little song I heard Nina singing to herself when she would be hanging up her curtains or doing her daily cleaning chores. I found it written among her papers:)

My name is Nina,
I am misunderstood
I live in an apple box,
it's fairly good

I think I am very pretty
but I have to be wary –
Some people don't like me
Because my tail isn't hairy

For all the little lab rats that
no-one ever gets to know….

Made in the USA
Middletown, DE
14 March 2019